Finding Chance

by Linda Benson

Illustrated by Nancy Lane

For my grandmother, who taught me how to play casino;
for my mother, who taught me how to walk in the woods; and
for my daughter, who taught me how to believe in myself

Thanks also to Lainee Cohen, my first and best editor, who
made the whole process so much fun; to Cheryl Coupè, my
friend and fellow writer for her wonderful insights; and to my
husband, who is always there for me

—L.B.

To Judith

—N.L.

Text copyright © 2006 by Linda Benson
Illustrations copyright © 2006 by Nancy Lane
under exclusive license to MONDO Publishing

For information contact:
MONDO Publishing
980 Avenue of the Americas, New York, NY 10018
Visit our web site at
www.mondopub.com
Printed in China
10 11 12   9 8 7 6 5 4 3

ISBN 1-59336-695-7
Designed by Jean Cohn

Library of Congress Cataloging-in-Publication Data
Benson, Linda, 1948- Finding Chance / by Linda Benson; illustrated by
Nancy Lane. p. cm. ISBN 1-59336-696-5 Twelve-year-old Alice, unhap-
py that she and her writer mother are always moving around, finds happiness
and more when they end up in California. [1. Moving, Household—Fiction.
2. Family life—Fiction. 3. Dogs—Fiction. 4. California—Fiction.] I.
Lane, Nancy, ill.   II. Title.   PZ7.B44726Fin 2006   [Fic]—dc22
2005036828

Contents

CHAPTER ONE

A Fresh Start

*A*lice smashed the brittle madrone leaves under her feet. She heard them crinkle as she walked, kicking the pieces out of her way. "Take your letter into town," her mom had said. "Give you something to do."

Yeah, right. As if there were anything to do in this dumb town. Fox Creek. What a stupid name for a town. Alice made up a poem as she headed reluctantly down the road.

> *Don't know anyone in this stinkin' place,*
> *No one even knows my face.*
> *Why'd we come here anyway?*
> *This summer's such a waste.*

They were always moving. Every time Alice started to get settled somewhere and began to make friends, her mom would hear of some new place. A great opportunity. A fresh start. But Alice decided she knew the real reason why they moved around so much. Her mother had restless feet.

Alice glanced sideways at the shabby cottages lining the roadway. She craned her neck up toward the shade of the steep hillsides. More cabins, some built on stilts, leaned out precariously from the side of the mountain. *Wonder what happens if they have one of those big earthquakes?* she thought.

I wish we could have stayed in Oregon. Sixth grade was going to be so cool this year. I should be hanging out with Emily and her friends. Instead, I'm walking down this country-bumpkin lane, toward this nowhere town with nobody in it that I even know.

Dear Emily,

California is not at all like I expected. We are staying in this funky old cabin. It is way up on top of a hill, and it looks like a hobbit house. Our water comes from the creek down below. It gets pumped up to a big tank above our cabin. We have a television, but it gets only three channels, and two of them are fuzzy. How are you? Do you still go to the mall? There is no such thing as a mall in this town. There is nothing around here but trees.

Please write back.

Your friend,
Alice

The pavement in front of Alice meandered slowly through sunny glens filled with tan oak and red madrone. Then it rounded a corner into the deep shade of a redwood grove. Ancient trees towered above her.

"It's only about a mile," her mom had said. "Take your letter. Go. It will be good for you."

"I don't want to go. What if I get lost? What if I can't find my way home? How come I can't get a cellphone?"

"Alice, you're almost 12 years old. You're not a baby anymore. How could you possibly get lost if you stay on the same road going both ways? Besides, I'm sure you're much safer here in this small town than you would be walking around the streets of Portland with your friends. And you know we can't afford a cell. Now go. Vamoose! I've got work to do, and I'm right in the middle of this chapter."

Mom's chapter. Mom's book. Right. . . Alice slunk out. The letter clutched in her hand was her only connection to Oregon—and the home she had left behind.

Sure seems like more than a mile to this town. Nobody in Portland would have walked a mile to the post office—they would have driven. Alice repeated the names of the roads that she passed. *Fawn Ridge Lane, Wild Trillium Road, Jacob's Creek Road, Baird's Crossing. Sounds like I'm in a wild jungle. What am I going to do all summer in this place?*

Alice stopped abruptly. There was a quick flash of movement to her right, but it was gone before she could identify it. Something white, or at least light colored, and bigger than a house cat. An involuntary shiver crept up her spine, and she walked faster. Alice had heard of cougar attacks, but she didn't think a wild animal would show up so close to town. But where was town? Alice quickened her steps, and relief washed over her when she noticed buildings up ahead.

The buildings weren't very impressive. The entire town of Fox Creek consisted of about two blocks of well-worn structures lining the country road. There were a few rows of older homes down along the river and an auto repair shop on the curve in the highway. *Don't blink, or you'll miss it.* That's what Alice and her mother used to say whenever they had driven through little podunk towns like this. She never thought she would actually have to live in one, even if she was in the sunny state of California.

Alice expected the post office to be a separate building. But all she saw was a tiny room tacked on to the side of Duncan's grocery, the only store in town. There was a mail receptacle out front, and an American flag waved overhead. Someone had planted bright pansies in a round wooden planter near the entrance. Alice held her letter tightly against her chest, not wanting to let go of her only connection to Emily and Portland. She climbed the broken concrete steps, pushed open the heavy door, and went inside.

CHAPTER TWO

Small Town Post Office

*A*lice glanced around the tiny space. The entire post office was no bigger than a bedroom. Stepping up to the counter, she felt a shyness overcome her. *I don't belong here,* she thought. *I don't know even one person in this whole town.*

"Well, good morning, dear." The booming voice of the postmistress filled the room, magnified by the close proximity of the walls. "I almost didn't see you standing there. Now, where in the world did you come from?"

Florence was written on her name tag. Alice didn't think she looked like a postmistress. She wore a light blue man's shirt with denim pants, and her hands were rough and calloused. Her close-cropped hair and the dirt under her fingernails made Alice think of a gardener.

Alice stammered. "From Fox Creek Road. I walked." She held up the letter addressed to Emily. "I need to mail this. Do you have stamps?"

Florence's wide smile lit up the room. "Oh, did you ever come to the right place. Do we have stamps! Honey, we have a whole collection of stamps."

Alice glanced around. She observed the row of post

office boxes and the single counter for addressing envelopes. She spotted a large community bulletin board sporting notices for garage sales, pickup trucks for sale, lost dogs, and even free roosters. No one else came through the door. "Whole collection?" she asked.

Florence pulled open a creaky drawer behind the counter. "Well, we have these stamps with United States flags on them. They are always popular."

"That would be fine...."

"But wait now. You've always got to pick out the stamps that you like best. That's half the fun of buying stamps, don't you think?"

"I guess." In every other post office Alice had been to, people stood in line impatiently. Alice watched as Florence—who seemed to have all the time in the world—carefully spread out the entire array on the counter.

"Well," she said. "You can have wildflower stamps. Aren't they just gorgeous?" Florence laid out more. "Then there are the new wildlife stamps. We've got mountain lions, wolves, and bobcats...."

"Are there any of those animals around here?" asked Alice, remembering the movement in the brush.

"Oh, I don't think so, honey. Not anymore. But there used to be a den of foxes—up on Fox Creek. That's how this town got its name."

"Oh." Alice was relieved, thinking of the walk back home on the same road that she took into town. Trying to act more grown-up, she changed the subject. "Do you have any stamps that say California on them?"

"Well, let me just see what I did with those last few state stamps." Florence shuffled her hand around in the

11

back of her drawer. "Here we go," she said. "We have just two left. They say, 'Greetings from California,' and they have a picture of a surfer on them. What do you think?"

"That would be perfect!" Alice said. "It's for my friend in Portland."

"Portland, Oregon? Is that where you're from? I knew I hadn't seen you here before."

"We just moved here."

"So, coming from a big city like that, you must be impressed with this metropolis we call Fox Creek." Florence snorted, her laughter shooting its way out through her nose.

Alice wasn't sure how to answer. She just shrugged.

"Give it time," said Florence. "Little towns grow on you after a while. And you don't have to be here very long to belong."

Belong. What does it feel like to belong?

Alice took her time picking out stamps. There wasn't anything else to do anyway. She finally chose two of the wildflower stamps—the trillium, and the Indian paintbrush. Then she took some American flag stamps and the last two California stamps to put on letters to Emily. She pulled a crinkled five-dollar bill out of her pocket.

"You like my pansies out front?"

Alice nodded, "They're nice."

She pasted a stamp on her letter to Emily and dropped it in the box labeled "Outgoing Mail." Pushing open the large wooden door, she nearly bumped into a man with long gray whiskers. Except for his grimy overalls, he could have passed for Santa Claus.

"Mornin', Florence," he burst out, loudly.

"Mornin', Payson."

Alice stood outside the post office, clutching her small bag of stamps. She smelled the damp aroma of the river across the highway. She wanted to explore what was left of the town, but it was incredibly hot. Alice wasn't used to the heat. Oregon had still been cool and rainy when they left in early June. She began the hike back up Fox Creek Road toward their cabin.

She hadn't gone far before sweat began to run down the back of her neck. And her feet hurt. She'd worn her brand-new cross trainers, which were rubbing a blister on her heel. Her mom had bought them for her in the mall. Alice knew they couldn't really afford them. But she wanted them badly, and her mom had given in.

Geez, it's hot out here, thought Alice. Back in Oregon, everything was still green with all the rain. But here in the strong California sun, all the bushes and wildflowers along the side of the road were turning dry and brittle. Everything looked completely different.

Ouch! Her shoes hurt her. She reached down and, slipping them off, began walking again. She could feel every little rock and pebble in the road, and the pavement burned the soles of her feet. When she approached the lane marked Baird's Crossing, she sat down briefly on the edge of the roadway to rest.

Alice pulled each foot up in turn and inspected it. Suddenly she froze. Florence had said there were no wild animals around here, but Alice heard something. It rustled in the underbrush behind her, as if ready to leap out at any moment.

13

CHAPTER THREE

Heron

*H*ey!"

Alice almost jumped out of her skin. Out of nowhere, a large girl came striding out of the bushes. Her round face was filled with an impish grin. "Did I scare you?"

Alice was so startled she could barely talk. "I th. . . thought you were a wild animal." That was all she could spit out.

Wearing a red and white tank top that was way too tight for her plump body, the girl had hair that was jet black, like the color you get out of a bottle of dye. She had on denim cutoffs and little flip-flop sandals. "Yeah, wild animal. That's me, all right. Never seen you around here before. Where'd you come from?"

"Why'd you jump out of the bushes like that?" asked Alice.

"Oh, I just wanted to see what you'd do. Where are you from?" she asked again. "Are you just here for the summer?"

"I don't know. We just got here." Still startled, Alice couldn't help staring at the girl. There was something

14

about her that was different from the kids that Alice had hung out with in Oregon.

"Where did you live before?"

"Portland," said Alice.

"Where's that?"

"In Oregon."

"Oh. Why'd you come here?"

Alice was getting tired of answering questions. "Are you writing a book, or what?"

"No, I just wanted to know."

"It was my mom's idea. She actually is writing a book. I guess she thinks we had to move out here in the California wilderness so she can get her book finished." Alice didn't know why her mom couldn't have finished her dumb book in Portland.

"Oh," said the strange girl. "Hey, want to go walk the rails?"

"The what?"

"The railroad tracks—they're just up here a little ways. Come on." She motioned up Baird's Crossing Road.

"But I'm barefoot," said Alice. "I got a blister on my heel. And my mom will probably get worried if I don't come back right away."

"It's okay. You won't be late. It's just right up here. Anyway, bare feet are better for balancing. You'll see."

Alice watched the long stride of the girl as she moved quickly away from her up the road. The road followed a small creek that tumbled out of the deepening woods just ahead. Alice didn't know what to do. Her feet hurt, and she still had to walk all the way home to the cabin.

15

Who is this girl? And how can there be railroad tracks out here in the middle of a forest? "Hey, wait up," she called as she jumped to her feet and skip-hobbled out onto Baird's Crossing Road.

Grasping her cross trainers in one hand and her stamps in the other, Alice tried to catch up to the girl. The pavement came to an end, and the road turned to gravel. "Ouch, ouch, ouch, OOUUCH. . . " she cried.

"Not very tough footed, are you?" The girl took a step or two back towards Alice. "Don't worry, I'll wait for you."

"Well, in Oregon nobody ever goes barefoot—until summer," Alice shot back. She tried to put her feet down normally. "It doesn't really get hot until then."

"Oh, it does get hot here. Everything starts drying up by the middle of May. The wildflowers are real pretty, though, in the early spring."

Alice limped along the road, trying to keep pace. "What's your n—?"

"I'm Heron," the girl said, as if reading her mind.

"Heron? Like the bird?" asked Alice.

"Yeah. My mom was really into weird names when I was born. Can you tell?"

Alice smirked. She had heard a lot of odd names for kids. But the name *Heron* seemed way off base for this strange, chubby girl. Alice kept her thoughts to herself as she struggled along beside Heron, trying to keep up. The road went around a bend to the right, leaving the singing creek and abruptly climbing a small hill, where it emerged onto a sunny plateau. And there, straight ahead of them, a set of railroad tracks crossed the road. Heron removed her red flip-flops and hopped up on the tracks barefoot. She spread her arms wide for balance, holding a sandal in each hand. As Heron carefully put one foot exactly in front of the other, Alice stifled a laugh. Standing on one foot at a time, Heron suddenly looked exactly like the large ungainly bird for which she was named.

"Come on! Try it." Heron called out as she inched her way along on the iron rails. Foot after foot, she was moving slowly towards a field of gigantic tree stumps.

"Where do these rails go?" Alice was still unsure about following Heron. "I have to be home soon."

"Where's home?" called Heron, glancing back over her shoulder.

"The end of Fox Creek Road," hollered Alice. Although this was the second time that she had told someone where she and her mom lived now, she wasn't convinced that it was home yet. "We're staying in this old cabin way up on top of a hill."

"Cool," said Heron. "Hey, I think I know which one it is. Up here a little ways, there's a trail through the forest that comes out right close to the place where you're living."

Alice tucked her package of stamps into the back pocket of her shorts. Holding a shoe in each hand to balance herself, she put one foot unsteadily on the iron rails of the old tracks. The rails were slicker than they looked and felt hot under her bare feet. "Ow!" she cried out. "How do you do this? They're hot!"

"Oh, your feet get tougher after a while." Heron walked in front of her on the tracks, gaining speed.

Alice was slower. The rails were shiny and smooth, and they had picked up the heat of the early summer afternoon. Alice felt her toes grip the metal. She put one foot hesitantly in front of the other and then repeated the process.

Heron called out instructions from ahead. "Don't look down—look straight ahead."

Heron and Alice made their way down the tracks like two exotic birds doing a rain dance. *One foot, two foot. Stick like glue foot.* Alice made up rhymes in her head to help with her balance.

Alice was just getting the hang of it—and almost keeping up—when suddenly she had a frightening thought. "Hey, Bird-Girl. What if. . . ?" She cupped her hands to her mouth and hollered down the tracks. "A big train isn't going to come roaring down on us, is it?"

CHAPTER FOUR

The Birthing Tree

*D*id you hear me?" All she could see was the raven black hair of the girl bobbing in front of her on the rails. Heron was moving farther ahead. Alice didn't know whether to follow or to put her shoes back on, blisters or no blisters, and turn back towards the cabin the way that she had come. That was beginning to seem like a good option, when suddenly Heron, just like a gymnast, pirouetted halfway around on the rails.

"What did you say? Rain? No, it doesn't ever rain here in the summer. Not in California. Not here. No way, no how." Heron was making elaborate gestures with her arms, imitating raindrops falling from the sky.

Alice burst into a giggling fit and almost lost her balance. "No, *train.* Are there any trains that come through here?"

"Nope." Heron shook her black head of hair. "No trains at all—not since the mill closed up."

"Is that what all those old shacks and stuff are back there?" Alice turned and pointed behind her. This time she did lose her balance and had to step off the tracks.

"Yep. The trains used to bring the trees out of the

forest and then haul the lumber away. But that was before I was even born. Now these tracks just sit here and rust," said Heron.

They had almost made their way through a sunny clearing. The stumps they passed loomed large on either side of them. "Those trees were HUMONGOUS," Alice said.

Heron stole a glance backward. "Yeah. Redwoods. Too bad they cut all those big ones down, huh?"

The tracks entered the woods again, and the two girls continued, foot by foot, balancing atop them. Thick brush grew right up to the sides of the forgotten rails, as if to swallow them back into the forest. The forest of tan oak and burly maples that surrounded them with its underbrush of salmonberry and wild huckleberry created a tunnel that was dark, shady, and inviting.

Alice had a very hard time keeping her balance. She tilted her head this way and that, growing dizzy in the process. She was glad for Heron's company, because her surroundings had suddenly become wild and junglelike. But there was a beauty to it—this denseness, the folds of the forest. It made her feel almost like a jungle animal herself, as if she could run off into the woods and somehow be free, able to choose her own path.

"Hey—we're almost to the trail. It's just up here past the birthing tree," cried Heron.

"The what?"

"The birthing tree," said Heron. "We've always called it that. It's a big old redwood with a hollowed-out stump. Once, me and my brothers found a wild cat in there."

"A cougar?" Alice had momentarily forgotten about

wild animals. She had been too busy pretending that she was one herself.

"No, not a cougar. Just a regular-size cat," said Heron. "But she was wild, and you couldn't catch her. She had a bunch of little tiny kittens in that tree. She ran out when we came up on her, carrying her kittens in her mouth. But she left one behind. We watched for a while, and called and called for the mother cat, but she never came back. So here was this pitiful little thing, mewing and squirming around in there with its eyes shut. So we took it home and gave it milk with an eyedropper."

"Did it live?" asked Alice.

"Oh, yeah. You should see him. He's huge. He's my cat—my big old sweetie pie. And guess what his name is?"

"What?"

"Stump," said Heron. "'Cause he's got no tail. And also 'cause of where he was born."

"Oh. I've seen a picture of that kind of cat in the library. Manx—is that what they're called?"

"Yeah, a minx cat," said Heron.

"No, not minx. Manx," insisted Alice. "They don't have tails."

"Minx, Manx—whatever. Hey, check this out. Right there, just like I told you." Heron motioned off to the right.

Alice stepped down from the rails. To the left, the rails continued into the forest, but became more overgrown with brush and almost impassable. But to the right, where Heron pointed, the branches parted. Through an almost imperceptible opening, sunlight

22

filtered down onto a little-used path.

Alice was amazed. Looking out through the small opening in the trees, she could see a grassy path that meandered into the distance. Alice felt like a wild deer. She wanted to explore this new route—to see where it led. She no longer felt the soles of her feet burning or the blister on her heel.

"Just like I said. There's the path that takes you home," said Heron.

"Home?"

"Yeah, just go up there a little ways, and it comes out on to Fox Creek Road. You're staying at the end of Fox Creek in that cabin way up on the hill, right?"

"Yeah," said Alice.

"Well, go. Hurry up, so your mom won't get mad."

Alice hesitated. "Aren't you going to show. . . ?"

But Heron was turning back now, ducking under the branches and heading towards town. And before Alice could even finish the thought in her head, Heron had disappeared around the bend.

Alice was alone in the clearing.

CHAPTER FIVE

The Library

*D*ear Emily,

Well, like I said, there's a lot of trees around here. Gigantic redwoods, and some with peeling red bark called madrone trees. Mom's working on her book all the time, and she wants me to go find "something to do." Yeah, right.

I did meet this one girl, though. Her name is Heron, like the bird. Weird, huh? She's one year older than me, and she taught me how to walk barefoot on the railroad tracks. Plus, she showed me a secret trail through the woods. I was scared at first. (I had to find my way home by myself.) But the trail came out right by our cabin, just like she said it would.

I miss you. Say hi to everyone for me. Please write back.

Your friend,
Alice

P.S. Do you know what teacher you'll have in the fall?
P.P.S. It's hot here. Not like Oregon.
P.P.P.S. It's so boring here that I am finally writing in my journal. I'm trying to write a poem. I'll send it to you if it turns out okay.

Alice was used to being by herself. She was an only child, and her mother, Nora, had been a writer for as long as she could remember. This time Nora was writing a book about Scotland. It was full of hills and dales and people speaking in a kind of language that was hard to read. Gaelic, or something like that.

It seemed as if her mother used to be more fun, but now she just plowed through the stacks of books piled up around the cabin, researching the history and customs of Scotland. "Can't we go do *something*, Mom? Like go to the beach? We *are* in California now."

"Soon, Alice. We'll do something fun. I promise." Nora looked tired as she glanced up from her work. "I just have to finish the first draft of this book. I'm on a deadline, darling. Sorry."

Alice wandered aimlessly around, pacing like a tiger. Then out behind the cabin she found a small weathered building that was so old it seemed to be growing from the hillside. It appeared to be a storeroom of some kind. Alice tried the door. At first it stuck and wouldn't budge. But with effort and with a groan from its rusty hinges, the door creaked open, scraping against the stone floor.

Alice peered inside. There was barely any light, and everything was covered with dust and cobwebs. It was

25

kind of creepy. Alice found some books in a corner and rummaged through them. Wiping her dusty hands on her pants, she glanced up. Hanging down from a broken shelf was some woven material. As Alice pulled on it, it fell into her hands. A hammock!

She dragged it out into the sunlight and gave it a good shake. Dirt flew over her head until she sneezed. But the hammock appeared intact, save for a small hole or two.

Where could she hang it? It was too hot in the sun. There were lots of trees around the cabin, but none seemed just right. The redwoods were too large to tie anything around.

As Alice looked for the perfect place, she noticed a tiny clearing in the hillside. Two large madrone trees, with paperlike red bark grew on either side. Alice tied one end of the hammock to each tree and clambered up into her newly found haven. It was perfect.

Alice went back to the cabin, found a pencil, and retreated into the hammock with her journal. She closed her eyes and heard the creek singing way down below, traveling toward the river—and then the ocean beyond. She began to write in her journal—just mumblings at first, and then the beginnings of words that seemed to flow together. The hammock soon became her refuge during those hot afternoons, a place to gather her thoughts.

One warm, lazy day, absorbed in her writing, Alice barely heard her mother come up behind her.

"Honey, I need to do some more research. Want to go check out the library in town?"

"Yeah, I guess."

"You guess? Alice, you love to go to the library. I thought you'd be excited."

Alice shrugged her shoulders. She had library cards that she had saved from almost every place they had lived. She could probably still go back to Portland, Salem, or even Eugene and check out a book to take home. Alice had kept all of her old library cards, even though they didn't live in those cities anymore. *You never know,* she thought. *The way we move around, we might move back someday.*

Nora drove into town, which took almost no time at all. They parked in front of a building that Alice hadn't noticed before. It had an old redwood-shingled roof that was covered with green moss at least one inch thick. Wild clover grew in an unbroken carpet beneath the big redwoods that lined the path to the front door. Tucked into a little glen where two creeks ran together, it looked like a summer cabin, except for the small wood-carved sign out front. It said, "Public Library." Alice figured there would be plenty of old history books for her mother in a place like this. But she didn't think that she would find anything that would appeal to her.

The windows of the library were ancient, and the floors were old red squares of peeling linoleum. Someone had tacked a worn rug down on one side of the room to make it a little more comfortable. "Come on, this will be fun," said Alice's mom.

Sometimes Nora McNeil could be so upbeat that it was positively annoying.

There was a poster on the door announcing story

hours for the little kids who were out of school for the summer. Alice was too old for that. She had read the whole series of C.S. Lewis books. Today she thought she might look for a book on trees or wildflowers. She wanted to know the names of the plants that she saw on the hillside around her. Maybe she could find a good fantasy book to keep her occupied in the long days ahead.

As they stepped into the room, a man looked up from behind the counter and smiled. Alice had been expecting a tidy woman with gray hair and glasses. Not this guy. With his slightly long hair and crooked grin, he looked more like a computer geek than someone who would be in charge of a library.

Nora filled out the forms for their library cards. Alice knew the drill: rent receipt, proof of address, or electric bill. Something to show that you lived somewhere. Librarians didn't loan books to just anybody.

"Two cards?" asked the man in the library. "For you and your daughter?"

Alice fidgeted and glanced around. It was quiet in the library, but she wondered if anyone else was in there. *Was there someone back in the aisles who might overhear?*

"Yes, there's just Alice and me. We make up the whole family," said Nora.

Alice had heard this many times before, but she still hated the way her mom said it. Like it was just fine to not have a husband and a father in their family. Other people had fathers who had left them, fathers that were mean, fathers who were nice people, or fathers who were divorced. But Alice had no father at all, and she hated it when people discovered that.

The man behind the counter just took it in stride, though. "Your address says Fox Creek Road," he said. "I'll bet you're staying in the old Cooper cabin up there. The one that gets its water from the creek down below."

"How did you know that?" Alice's mother swung her full head of dark, wavy hair around as she talked. Her eyes sparkled.

Alice ducked down one of the aisles. Her mother was acting weird. Like, too friendly, already.

"Oh, everybody knows almost everything in this little town. We basically all watch out for one another. I'm Ned Felton, and I work here four days a week. The rest of the time, I like to think that I'm an artist, trying to get some of this beauty down on canvas." He laughed.

"Yes, it is lovely here," said Alice's mother. "These mountains just bring something out in you."

Alice pretended to be finding a book on the bottom shelf. She listened as her mother began telling this complete stranger practically everything.

"I'm Nora McNeil," she heard. "This is—well, my daughter Alice is around here somewhere." Alice hunkered down lower.

"I'm a writer," Nora continued. "I'm working on a novel that's set in Scotland, and, well, it's getting there. Alice and I came down from Oregon for the summer. We got a great deal on the Cooper cabin, and I thought a quiet place would be just the ticket for me to get this book finished. You know—just looking out the window gives me inspiration to write. Funny how that is. Very different from listening to the noise in a big city."

Alice tried her best to slip away toward the nonfiction section. Her mother caught sight of her, and, with an arm around her shoulder, nudged her toward Ned up for an introduction. "This is Alice. She wasn't too happy about moving down from Portland, but I think she'll like it after a while. You'll see her in here a lot—she's quite a reader." Nora reached over and ruffled the top of Alice's short brown hair with her hand, brushing the bangs back out of her eyes.

Alice ducked. She hated it when her mom did that. It made her feel like a baby. And she felt embarrassed when Nora talked about her, especially when she did it in front of people that they barely knew.

Ned put his hand out toward Alice. "Nice to meet you, Alice. If you need help finding any books, just let me know."

"Okay, I will." Alice shook his hand. She'd read somewhere that you can tell a lot about people from their handshakes. Ned's was firm.

Her mom began a long conversation about Scotland and the patterns of dialect, and Ned led her over toward the history section. Alice searched the shelves for books on wildflowers. She found two that described plants growing in the redwood forest, and then she headed for the fiction section. A shelf marked "Poetry" caught her eye, and she added two books of poems to her small collection. *Just for inspiration,* she thought.

Alice heard her mom talking up a storm with the librarian. It was kind of weird. Nora didn't know too many men and never went on dates. Not that Alice could ever remember. But there they were, just chatting away

in the history section like old friends. Talking about nature, and the traffic in Portland, and the advantages of small town living, and a bunch of other stuff. Alice kept her nose in the bookshelves, pretending to be reading.

It took forever to get all their books checked out. There was no computer, so Ned had to stamp the inside of every book with the due date using an old ink stamp pad. *I guess it is a cool library, even if does smell like ancient Scotland in here.* Ned held the door open for them, and as Alice balanced her stack of books, she grabbed a flyer near the front entrance. She hastily shoved it inside the top book. It said, "Summer Poetry Contest—contestants wanted."

CHAPTER SIX

Talking About Dads

D*ear Emily,*

Well, here goes: (My first poem)
   Sunlight filters down through the leaves
   Making pretty patterns that stir with the breeze.
   The creek sings a song all the way to the sea
   Running over ripples, running wild and free.
   I walk the paths of the forest trees.
   I feel the forest all around me.

So, will I make a great poet (or poetess)? There's going to be a poetry contest at the library here, so I guess I need to try and write some poems. The library is really old and little and kind of cool. There are big trees all around it and two creeks out back. I'm trying to read about the plants and trees around here—there's lots of them in the forest. Wish you could come visit me—we could go for a hike.

Your friend,
Alice

Alice wished that Emily would write back. She wanted someone to tell her if her poetry was any good or not, and she wanted to know what was happening with her friends in Portland. She had gone to David Douglas Elementary for only one year, but she had liked it there. That was before her mom had the brilliant idea to move to California. "We can stay in a cabin, Alice! In the woods. What could be more wonderful!"

"The woods? What am I going to do there? What about my friends? Emily and I are hoping to be in the same class next year and. . . " Tears of frustration had sprung from Alice's eyes. Her mom hadn't even listened to her.

Nora had gotten a dreamy look on her face. "We'll be living right in the middle of nature. It'll be a great experience for both of us. You'll love it, darling. I just know you will."

Alice had slunk back into her room. It hadn't really mattered what she thought. Nora had her mind made up. Suddenly they had moved to California—just like that. And now here they were in the cabin, with nothing but trees all around. . . .

"Hey, Portland Girl! Tender Foot. Are you up there?" Alice sprang from her reverie and glanced down the stone stairway to the bottom of the driveway. She saw the chubby girl with the jet black hair taking the steps, two at a time. It was Heron, who was at the top of the hill before Alice could even answer. "Want to play cards?"

"Cards?" Alice hesitated. She hadn't even seen Heron since the day they walked the railroad tracks.

Now here she was, like they were best friends.

Heron pulled out a well-used deck of cards from her hip pocket. She began moving them briskly from hand to hand, shuffling them.

"Ever play casino?" Heron asked.

"No. What's that?"

"A card game. It's cool. Where do you want to play? In the house?" asked Heron.

Alice thought about her mom, who was working diligently in the living room on her "next chapter." "No," she said. "Let's play outside."

"Okay," said Heron. "How about right here?" She sat abruptly on a flat rock. She took a branch, sweeping the leaves away to create a level playing area.

Alice folded her thin legs crossways and sat down opposite Heron. Heron dealt each of them four cards and then placed four more cards in the middle, face up. The rules were fairly simple, and Alice learned quickly. "Building sixes, building eights, big casino," they called out in turn as they each gathered in their cards.

"I've never even heard of this game," said Alice. "I bet nobody in Portland ever heard of it either."

"I learned it from my grandma," said Heron. "She knew lots of games."

Heron began showing up regularly at the cabin. She would appear suddenly at the bottom of the hill, sometimes singing, sometimes calling up to Alice.

Alice began to look forward to her visits. Heron taught her how to play gin rummy, knock, and black-jack. Since neither one of them had money to bet with, they used acorns instead. They would gather them from under the oak trees growing beside the cabin on the steep hills and count them out into even piles before they started.

In the bottom drawer of the cabin's kitchen, Alice found an old cribbage board made out of a deer antler. There was a deck of cards attached to it with a rubber band, but she didn't know how to play. Heron did. She taught Alice the rules of cribbage—how to count the cards and move the pegs up and down the board.

Sometimes the two of them walked along Fox Creek, which ran in the rugged ravine down below the cabin. Alice was getting good at balancing barefoot on the rocks sticking up out of the bubbling water. The soles of her feet became tough with hard calluses and clung to the slippery rocks with ease.

"Does your mom know that you're up here?" asked Alice one day. Hopping from rock to rock across the creek, she stole a backward glance at Heron.

"Yeah, and it's fine with her. She's glad if I have somewhere to go while she's working."

Heron skipped across the rocks to the other side of the creek and sat down on the mossy bank. "My brothers are always working, surfing, or somewhere."

"Surfing?" asked Alice. She hadn't even seen the ocean yet. Nora had been too busy writing to take Alice anywhere exciting, except to Fox Creek. And that was a pretty boring place.

"Yeah. The beach is only about 20 miles from here. I'm going to go hang out there every day as soon as I can drive."

"Where does your mom work?" asked Alice.

"She waits tables at the Captain's Club. It's a seafood place down in Maple Beach. She doesn't care where I go during the day as long as I'm home before dark. Sometimes she calls to check on me. Sometimes she doesn't."

"My mom always wants to know exactly where I am at all times," said Alice. "If I go into town, I have to come right back. Where's your dad? Is he home?"

"Yeah, right. Mom ran him off after the last time he showed up drunk. He was yelling and stuff. My mom got a restraining order. Now he doesn't come around any more," said Heron.

"Don't you miss him?"

"No. Well, sort of. I miss the way he used to be, a long time ago before he started drinking."

"At least you have a dad," said Alice.

"Everybody has a dad. Otherwise you'd never be born," said Heron. "Where's yours at, anyway?"

"I don't know for sure," said Alice.

"Have you ever seen him?"

"Once, maybe. But I think I was too young to remember." Alice sometimes had a faraway feeling of a tall, dark-haired man holding her. But it seemed to come from long ago, and she didn't know whether to trust her memory or not.

"What's your mom say? Have you asked her?"

"Yeah, a few times. She just says I might as well not have one. End of subject."

"Well, that's ridiculous. What does she mean by that? I think you better ask her again," said Heron.

"Last time I asked, she got sort of angry, and I

figured it just wasn't worth talking about. Anyway, it's always been just me and my mom. We move around a lot. We've lived in Portland, Salem, Eugene, and Beaverton, and that's just in Oregon. Before that, we lived in Washington, and in Colorado for one summer, and. . . well, I forget. I've been to a bunch of schools. I change schools at least once a year."

"Sounds exciting, if you ask me." Heron separated the strands of her hair with her fingers. "I wish I could do something to get out of this stupid little town."

"Well, moving around is lousy. You hardly ever make friends."

"I'm your friend," said Heron.

"No, that's not what I mean," said Alice. Her stomach twisted in a knot. She hadn't meant to hurt Heron's feelings. "It's just that we'd been in Portland for almost the whole school year, and I was finally starting to know some kids. We even went to the movies together a couple of times. There isn't even a movie theater in Fox Creek."

"That's true. It *is* a dinky little town. But sometimes we go over to the drive-in at Forest Glade. Maybe you could go with us sometime."

"That would be cool," said Alice. She was glad that she had recovered from that rough part with Heron. So far, Heron was the only friend that she had here in Fox Creek. Well, unless you counted Florence at the post office. And Ned, that librarian guy.

Heron jumped up then, gushing with a new idea. "Hey, got any bacon?"

CHAPTER SEVEN

Settling In

*D*ear Emily,

Yesterday Heron and I caught crawdads. We sat down by a deep hole in the creek where the water is dark and still. We cut bacon into little pieces and tied them on the end of a string. Then we dangled them in the water—down close to the rocks at the bottom, where the crawdads hide. You have to sit real quiet and not talk at all, which is hard. Anyway, here come these things with long claws slithering out. They look like lobsters, only smaller. They come out with their big pincers trying to latch on to the bacon. I guess they can smell it, even underwater. They are so interested in that bacon that once they get ahold of it, they won't let go. You can just drag those crawdads all the way out of the creek. We put them in a bucket of water and carried them all the way up the steps to the cabin. My arms were sore! Heron says some people cook them and eat them. My mom sort of freaked out, though, when I told her about that. She said we should throw them back. She felt sorry for them. I'm going to keep mine in the bucket for a little while. They're cute.

How come you haven't written to me? The deadline for the poetry contest is August 25th, but I don't know if my poems are any good. Please write back and tell me what you think.

Your friend always,
Alice

In her cozy bed in the cabin, Alice sometimes woke to a misty fog drifting by her window. It reminded her of Oregon weather—cloudy and cool. She found herself looking forward to the warmth of the day, when the fog burned off and gave way to lovely sunshine by midmorning. The sun felt good against her skin, and she was getting a "California tan." She welcomed errands that gave her a chance to walk into town.

Alice began to recognize the plants and trees and wildflowers that she found along the way. She could name madrone, monkey flower, and huckleberry, as well as manzanita and wild lilac. Along the shady banks of Fox Creek, she discovered wild lady ferns, maidenhair ferns, and giant chain ferns.

Sometimes the sound of a woodpecker *peck-peck-a-pecking* against a tree deep in the forest called out to Alice. Standing still to listen, she searched the forest canopy, waiting for the sight of its red head bop-bopping back and forth, searching for bugs in a rotted-out tree.

Alice's heart gradually filled with the great beauty of

her surroundings. She carried her journal everywhere now, and frequently paused to jot down a word or phrase—sometimes even a whole poem.

Alice often took the normal route toward town—down the crooked road along Fox Creek and past all of the houses perched on the hillsides. She had never seen anything remotely resembling a cougar or a fox spring from the bushes—not since her first walk into town. As she grew bolder and braver, Alice sometimes chose the back way. Down the secret trail through the forest, past the birthing tree where Heron's cat was born, and along the railroad tracks to Baird's Crossing Road, which entered town near the post office and Duncan's market.

Something about the birthing tree intrigued her. Alice made it a habit to stop and look inside. It was silly, really, because nothing had been in that hollow place in the old redwood for a long time. But Alice liked to imagine that she would find something there. A cat, like Heron found. Or maybe even a dog.

If Alice had a dog, the two of them could go for walks all over these woods. She would have company and something to protect her. Alice's mother had never liked dogs. She said they were too much "extra responsibility." And that landlords wouldn't rent to you. Alice didn't care. *A dog would love it out here in the country,* she thought. *It could be my dog. My very own.* It would probably never happen, though. And besides, who knew how long they would even remain in Fox Creek?

One sultry morning in July, Alice had been hanging around the house, hoping that Heron would show up. There had been no cooling fog this morning, and the day

was going to be a scorcher. Nora was working like a madwoman on her book, trying to meet her deadline. Alice was restless.

"Honey, would you go into town for me? I'm on a roll here with this chapter, and I really don't want to stop. We need a few items at the store."

Alice didn't mind—she had library books to return and a letter to mail. She shoved her books inside her backpack, heaving it up onto her shoulders. As she got to the bottom of their hill, Alice felt the heat rise off the pavement of Fox Creek Road. *It's almost too hot.* She decided to take the shady forest trail into town, even though it was a bit longer, but the canopy of trees offered little respite from the sweltering heat.

If only Mom would quit writing so much and take me to the ocean to play in the water! Twenty miles, that's how far Heron said it was. Wonder how long it would take to walk there? Too long. Alice could imagine the cool breakers pounding on the beach, even if she hadn't seen them yet. She created rhymes in her head—about water and waves, and hot summer days.

Alice was almost at the birthing tree. Suddenly she stopped short in her tracks, startled. The hair prickled on the back of her neck—an eerie feeling. Something darted quickly in front of her and jumped into the thick underbrush to hide.

CHAPTER EIGHT

Who's There?

I did not imagine that," Alice said out loud. She walked cautiously a few steps forward and poked her head inside the old hollow of the birthing tree. There were fresh marks there in the middle of the cool, dark earth, as if something had recently been scratching. *Was something sleeping in there?* Whatever it was, it had sensed her presence and left, just as she rounded the bend.

Alice retraced her footsteps to the trail. She started toward town, quickening her steps. She was glad when she reached the sunny clearing of the old mill site. She practically ran down Baird's Crossing Road, her book bag banging against her back. By the time she got to the post office, her breath was escaping in hard gasps.

"Whoa, young lady—it's too hot to be racing around. What gives?" said Florence, looking up from the pile of mail she was sorting.

Alice wiped the sweat off her forehead. It was partly from the heat of the day and partly from feeling frightened. "I just came down the trail from the old mill. I saw something running into the woods," she said.

"Something? Like a person?"

"No, it was small. And white, and it had long hair. I think I've seen it before, at the beginning of summer. Out on Fox Creek Road." Alice caught her breath, remembering her very first walk into town.

"Did it look like a fox?" asked Florence.

"I don't know. Maybe. Are foxes white?" asked Alice. "It came from the birthing tree. It had been scratching around in there. I practically ran all the way here."

"The birthing tree?" Florence looked puzzled for a moment, then her broad face widened into a smile. "Oh, you mean that old redwood with the rotted-out core where Heron found her kitten. I surely thought that little thing would die without its mother. But he made it. He's a big old cat now. Do you think it was a cat?"

"No, it was way bigger than a cat, " Alice responded.

"Was it bigger than a bread box?" Old Payson appeared out of nowhere. He was always hanging around the post office, teasing Florence. His overalls looked as if they hadn't been washed in a month, but Alice liked his eyes, which crinkled when he spoke. "What are we playing, 20 questions?" he asked.

"Well, something was scratching around in that old redwood," Alice repeated. "And then I saw something white slink into the bushes, and I. . . "

"It might have been a fox," said Florence. "But I'd be kind of surprised that it would den up so close to town. Must have been something wild, though, to run off when it caught your scent. Or a dog—what do you think?"

"Probably a coyote, more than likely," said Payson. He winked at Florence. "Or maybe that scrawny little dog that's been hanging around behind the market.

46

"A dog?" asked Alice.

"Kind of a mangy-looking, little white one," said Payson. "It's been here for a while. Somebody must've dumped it off out there on the highway. It'll probably get run over if it don't starve first."

Alice mailed her letters and walked quickly to the library. Then she dropped her books in the return box and hurried back toward Duncan's market.

Alice found the groceries on her mother's list and reached deep into the freezer box for a chocolate fudge bar. A giant swamp cooler rumbled from the corner, and Alice would have liked to hang around inside where it was cool. But she felt a sense of urgency—something pulling her back outside.

She paid for her groceries and hastened out the back door. Alice could feel the heat swell up against her. She sucked slowly on her ice cream, feeling the coolness on her tongue, and she tried to decide where a lost and hungry dog might be on a day like today.

Alice saw some movement from behind the big green Dumpster at the corner of the parking lot. She walked slowly toward it, and a thin white dog darted away from her and ran under the building. Its hair was matted into clumps, but Alice could see the outline of its ribs. Could this pathetic creature be what she had seen in the bushes? The thing that had given her such a fright?

Alice squatted in the shade at the corner of the market and peered into the shadows. After the blinding sunlight, she could barely see anything. She waited quietly for her eyes to adjust and held out her hand. "Come here, sweetie. Don't be afraid. Are you lost?"

CHAPTER NINE

A Mission

*D*_{ear Emily,}

Guess what? I found a dog. The poor little thing has been hiding under the grocery store. I think it's a girl, and someone might have dumped her out of a car. Isn't that awful? Yesterday I was calling and trying to get her to come out, and she was wagging her tail and crawling on her belly towards me. Then some noisy kids came out of the store, and she ran behind the garbage can and hid. I'm going to start taking some food to her every day. Her name is Chance—well, that's what I'm calling her, anyway.

How are things in Portland? Oh, yeah, I'm still thinking about the poetry contest, but I'm chicken to enter it.... Baaak, Baaak.

Your friend,
Alice

Alice now developed a regular routine. She decided it was her job to make a trip to town every morning. If Nora didn't have an errand for her to run—like checking the mail at the post office or picking up something at the store—Alice would make up some excuse to go. Instead of the usual route down Fox Creek Road, Alice chose the secret trail through the woods.

As the dappled shade of the forest path opened toward the old mill site, Alice passed the birthing tree. Each day she knelt down and cautiously searched for new tracks inside the opening or for the damp smell of freshly turned earth. The few leaves that were scattered there looked as if they had been slept on. She was sure now that something was using the hollow space in the old tree during the night. Was it Chance?

Every day Alice searched for the little dog. Now she had a mission—a reason to be here for the summer.

Nora noticed the change. "Hey, kiddo, you seem a little happier these days."

"Yeah, maybe." Alice quickly ducked out of the house without going into details. She didn't want to talk about the dog to her mother. Nora wouldn't understand. If she knew, she might spoil it by saying, "No dogs. Period." Alice didn't want to risk it.

Some days Alice found the frightened dog curled up in the cool shade under the market. Alice found an old margarine container and started putting stale slices of bread or cookies in it. She saved her roast beef sandwich from lunch and snuck it into town in her pocket. She got bacon out of the refrigerator, pretending she was going to use it to catch crawdads. Instead, she brought it to

Chance, who wolfed down every bite of food as if it were her last.

Alice found an old rusty pail near the Dumpster. She rinsed it out and, using the green hose from the back door of the market, filled it with water. Squatting on the hot pavement behind the back door of the grocery store, Alice cajoled, "Come here, little dog. Come see what I have for you."

Chance began to recognize Alice. Sometimes she crept from her hiding place, her belly to the ground, accepting a piece of food from Alice's outstretched hand. On other days the dog sat huddled under the store, too frightened to come out. Only after Alice walked completely around to the front of the building would the dog approach the food and eat. It was frustrating, but Alice didn't give up. She had to get the dog to trust her.

Alice's worries about Chance left an unsettled feeling in her stomach. She knew what it felt like to be in a strange place. *At least I have enough to eat,* she thought. After Alice had taken care of the dog, she often found herself at the library. She was a fast reader, and so every few days she went back to return her books and pick out new ones. Sometimes her mother had a request for Ned, the librarian, to order reference material for her novel.

Ned was okay. He wasn't nosy, and he didn't ask her questions about how long they were staying or where they came from. He wanted to know what kind of books Alice liked to read. It made her feel important—like her opinion counted for something.

After a particularly promising morning with Chance,

when the wary dog almost let Alice scratch the top of her head, Alice headed to the library. She sat on the floor in the back of the cozy room and dragged an over-sized book into her lap. *Breeds of Dogs,* it was called. Flipping through the pages, she studied the pictures intently, trying to imagine what kind of dog Chance might be. *Part terrier. Maybe some Old English sheepdog, only smaller. She'd have a pretty, curly coat if I could give her a bath and brush the snarls out of her.*

Alice wanted to bring the book home. The library actually had a lot of books about dogs—how to train them, how much to feed them, and what to do if they had puppies. But Alice didn't want her mom to be suspicious about her frequent trips to town. So she sat on the floor and read.

Ned always let her read for as long as she wanted. The library became a place of refuge. A place in which to dream. *I wish we didn't have to leave Fox Creek, so I could always come to this library. I wish we didn't have to move again. I wish I could get Chance to follow me home, and then she would be my very own dog. I wish that I could become a famous writer of poems.*

Ned shoved an old oak cart down the aisle at the back of the room, shelving books. He stopped when he came to Alice.

Alice forced herself out of her reverie and spit out a question before she lost her nerve. "How many people have entered the poetry contest?"

"Well, we've had a few people sign up so far. Why? Have you written some poetry?"

CHAPTER TEN

Real Talent

*W*ritten some poetry? This was the question she'd feared. She hadn't shared her poems with anyone but Emily, who was in Portland and hadn't responded to her letters. "I've been trying. I've written a few."

"Would you like to enter them in the contest? It might be a good experience."

"Oh, no. I don't think they're good enough. I mean. . . I'm just learning to write poems," said Alice. She felt trapped now, and she wished that she hadn't asked.

"I could look at them first, if you'd care to have my opinion," said Ned. "I'm not going to judge the contest. That's done by the English teacher at the high school. But I promise to tell you what I honestly think."

Alice contemplated that idea for a moment. "Maybe. Well, okay. I haven't even let my mom see them, or anyone, 'cause I don't think they're any good."

"You can bring them by anytime," said Ned. "I'd be happy to read them."

"Oh, I have them right here in my journal," said Alice. "That way I can write them down whenever I get the inspiration."

"Spoken like a true writer," said Ned. "Maybe you take after your mother more than you realize."

No, I'm not like my mother. Alice gritted her teeth together at the mere suggestion. *Not at all. I don't like to just pack up and move any old chance I get.* That's what Alice wanted to say. But what was the point? She fumbled through her backpack. "Mostly I just write letters to my friend back in Portland."

From the bottom of her backpack, Alice pulled out two library books that she needed to return, the mail that she had picked up from the post office box, two stale pieces of bread that she was going to leave for Chance, lip gloss, three sticks of chewing gum, and a short stub of a pencil with the eraser chewed off. She finally pulled out her journal. The corners were dog-eared, and the pages were stuck together in places. Alice hurriedly opened it and set it up on the counter—before she chickened out and before someone else came into the library.

Ned pushed aside a stack of books on the counter, picked up her journal, and began to read.

> *Small and free*
> *larger than life*
> *under the sunlight I grow.*
> *Like a bird I fly*
> *with wings spread wide*
> *where I'll go I don't know.*

Alice fidgeted. She felt clammy underneath her armpits. Why was he taking so long?

"Opens up some possibilities," said Ned. "Any more?"

"Yeah, here's another one," Alice replied. "I wrote this when I walked up to the top of our hill." She found the page in the journal and showed it to Ned.

> *Alone and free, I stretch out my wings*
> *Where I'll fly nobody knows.*
> *Like the hawk above me, like the dust below,*
> *I'll go with the wind wherever it blows.*
> *Nobody knows.*
> *Nobody knows.*

"Sounds kind of lonely and hopeful all at the same time," offered Ned. "Do you have more like these?"

Alice showed several more poems to Ned, and he read each one slowly. It was agony waiting for him to finish.

Finally, he nodded his head and smiled. "Good."

"Here's one that I just wrote—about Chance, a little dog that's hiding under the grocery store. She's kind of my secret project. I've been feeding her, and she finally let me pet her. I think I even know where she sleeps at night," said Alice. She handed the paper to Ned.

> *Lonely and scared*
> *Alone in a new world*
> *No one to love you*
> *and no one to trust*
> *Reach out for love*
> *So you won't be alone*
> *Take a big chance*
> *And you might find a home.*

Ned raised his eyebrows. "About a dog named Chance...," he said.

"Want to see the rest of them?" Alice flipped through the pages and showed him poems she had written on the lonely days when they first arrived in Fox Creek. She showed him the poems that she had sent to Emily, poems written down by the creek, and poems written in the forest.

Ned took his time. Alice could tell that he was reading carefully, because sometimes he stopped in the middle of a sentence, as if savoring a thought. She searched his face while he read, trying to find some measure of her literary merit. Finally, he spoke. "Alice, I think these poems show real promise. I think that you should enter them in the poetry contest at the end of this month."

"But I'm not really a poet. I'm just learning."

"I think you are a poet, Alice. You see, real poetry comes straight from the heart. There are lots of people who can make words rhyme. But that's just rhyming. True poetry is being able to capture a feeling with words. You've done that with these poems, Alice. I think that you have real talent."

Real talent. Alice beamed.

CHAPTER ELEVEN

At the Beach
With Mom

*D*ear Emily,

I think I will enter the poetry contest, but I'm still scared. Ned, the librarian, said he thought my poems were good. He said they showed promise and that I have "real talent!"

Mom said she was going to take a break from writing so much and take me to the beach. Finally! It should be warm there. (Not like Oregon.)

Oh yeah, I've been feeding Chance every day. I even wrote a poem about her. She looks a little better— not so skinny. Her belly is rounder. She lets me scratch her on the head now if I move really slow. I wish she could be my very own dog.

Your friend, the famous poet,
Alice

The windows were completely down, and Alice felt the warm air rush past her, messing up her dark brown hair. For once she was spending the day with her mother, and they were finally going to the beach. The narrow back road twisted and turned underneath the towering presence of ancient redwoods and around steep banks filled with the long tendrils of waving green ferns. So many colors of green. Alice inhaled deeply, wanting to draw into her lungs every bit of the pure and rich forest air.

Nora had been so engrossed in her book that it seemed as if it had been forever since they had been on a mother–daughter outing. They had packed beach towels, sunscreen, and a cooler filled with soda, water, sandwiches, and potato chips. Her mother found a big, floppy hat in the closet of their cabin. She said it was for protection against the strong California sun. Alice pulled an old baseball cap down low over her forehead. It said, "San Francisco Giants," on it. They seemed like two silly girls going on an adventure.

This is the way it used to be, Alice mused, *before Mom started working so hard, trying to meet her silly deadlines.* They used to have a lot of fun together. It had always been just the two of them for as long as Alice could remember. Nora McNeil had worked at quite a few part-time jobs, besides being an author, trying to make ends meet. But she was home a lot, too. They would go to garage sales on weekends, looking for bargains. They would find free concerts and bring home stacks of library books and go for nature walks in the parks of the various towns where they had lived. Left on her own so much this summer, in her new surroundings, Alice had almost forgotten about the enjoyable times they spent together.

Lost in her reverie, Alice smelled the ocean before she saw it. The breeze turned sharp and salty, and she realized that they were practically there. Then she could hear it—the waves crashing, slapping against the shore. And then she saw it—the vast blue-green water of the Pacific, with perfect whitecaps rolling one after another onto a long stretch of sand.

"Look, Alice." Her mom was pointing at a long pier built on pilings, stretching far out over the water.

"Can we drive out there?" asked Alice.

"I guess so. The cars are all headed that way."

As they maneuvered their vehicle out along the wooden planks, Alice got the weirdest sensation in the pit of her stomach. She heard the wheels of the car—*thump, thump, thump,* as they rolled from board to board. The wood seemed to give a little, and far down below them the waves were rolling, tumbling constantly toward the shore. It almost made her seasick.

People were lined up along the sides of the pier with fishing poles, their lines strung down into the water below. Little kids with pails of bait and half-eaten bags of french fries, old grandmas in short flowered muumuus, and surfers with sun-bleached hair and skin-like leather all paraded up and down the edge of the pier as if they were right at home. The air smelled like fish and seaweed. Alice heard a roar and glanced down as a giant wave broke beneath her. The sharp spray of saltwater grazed her cheek. *Welcome to California!* She smiled.

Nora stopped the car to look around. They got out and put a quarter in a large telescope mounted to the railing. Alice and her mom took turns looking at the sea lions barking on the rocks in the distance. "Having fun?" asked her mom.

Alice nodded.

"I'm glad you got your smile back. You've been mad at me ever since we left Portland."

Alice stuck her tongue out playfully.

"Come on, goose. Let's go get a spot on the beach before they're all gone."

Alice got back in the car. Her mom hadn't called her "goose" in a long time. It was a baby name really, but today Alice didn't mind.

They drove to an area that said, "Beach Parking," and carried all their stuff down along the wide expanse of sand. Alice kicked off her sandals and felt the fine grains of sand tickle the bottoms of her feet. She could feel the heat burning her bare soles, but she could tolerate it. Her feet were finally getting tough.

"Where do you want to sit?"

Alice shrugged her shoulders, turning her palms faceup. "I don't know. Let's go down by the water."

They picked a spot close to where the waves broke along the shore. Alice dropped the beach blankets she was carrying and ran out into the water to cool off her feet. It was a little cold at first, but it felt good with the warm sun streaming down on her. Way different from Oregon, where the water never got warm enough for swimming. She splashed the water up against her body. *Perfect*, she thought.

Alice stood in the ankle-deep water, watching her mother lay out towels and blankets on the sand. Nora unfolded her beach chair and massaged sunscreen meticulously into her fair skin. "Come on, darling. Better get some of this stuff on you. You don't want to get a bad burn, do you?"

"Okay. . . I'm coming." Alice wasn't worried about getting burned. She loved the sun, and in the California rays, she was already getting a surfer-girl tan.

Standing in the breaking waves, Alice took a hard look back at her mother. *We sure don't look alike.* Her mother was tall and elegant, with pale skin and wavy hair falling down to her shoulders. Alice's stick-straight figure had not yet begun to develop, and her hair was straight as a board. No curl whatsoever. Getting it chopped into a short bob always seemed like the best solution.

Alice came running out of the water and shook herself off like a wet puppy. Rustling around in the knapsack for a sandwich, she blurted out a question before she could stop herself. "Mom, am I adopted?"

CHAPTER TWELVE
Alice's Father

*A*dopted? Whatever gave you that idea?"

"Well, I never get sunburned, like you. I don't have wavy hair, like you," she said. "And I don't have a dad, or at least you've never told me anything about my dad, so I figured out I must be adopted. Am I?"

"Alice, sit down," said her mother. "First of all, you are not adopted. I don't know where in the world you came up with that idea. And I really hate to wreck this gorgeous day by even discussing this, but I see that you need to know about your father."

"What about my father?" asked Alice. She crossed her arms over her chest. Whatever remained of her light-hearted mood evaporated when she saw the serious look on her mother's face.

"He was not a very nice person." Nora's words came haltingly, as if she was trying to measure out what she was going to say.

Alice sat cross-legged on the blanket. The heat of the day suddenly pressed in on her, choking her.

"He wasn't ready to be a father—wasn't fit to be a father. But I didn't find that out until you were almost

born. We were young and silly back then, and I honestly thought we were in love." Her mother stopped for a moment.

Alice saw tears well up in Nora's eyes, as her mother continued.

"Even though we were married, he didn't want to stick around and help raise you. And he had a mean streak that didn't come out at first, not until he found out we were going to have a baby. Have you." Nora put her face in her hands.

Alice waited.

"I didn't want you to be exposed to that, to have you grow up around that. I wanted you to be happy—to have a happy life. I've tried to make a good life for you on my own, Alice. It hasn't always been easy."

"Where is he now?" asked Alice. "Do you even know?"

"No. He's long gone."

Alice felt overwhelmed with this information. She saw that her mom needed a hug, but Alice wasn't ready. "So why do we keep moving around so much? What if he's looking for us?"

"Alice, I gave up waiting for that to happen a long, long time ago. Trust me, he's not looking for us." Nora's face twisted, as if it still hurt to think about it. "I guess all those old memories just finally got to me, and I figured we could make a new start somewhere else, just you and me. And then we moved again, and. . . well, I've never found a really good place to stay. You know, a place where it seemed like we should settle down permanently."

But Alice wasn't finished. "Was he tall, or was he short?" she asked. "My dad."

"He was tall, honey," said Nora. Alice couldn't tell if her mom was laughing or crying. "A big, tall jerk, who didn't have the sense to want a daughter as wonderful as you turned out to be."

"What was his name then? His real name?" It seemed like an important thing to know.

"Harold."

"Harold?" Alice wrinkled her nose and stammered. "H—his name is Harold?"

Nora nodded, then smirked, and the two of them giggled.

Alice pulled her baseball cap down low against her eyes. She had more questions, but they could wait. She chewed on the inside of her lip and waded into the shallow waves of the wide Pacific Ocean.

CHAPTER THIRTEEN

Hawk's-eye View

*A*lice followed her mother's footsteps, breathing heavily as she climbed the stone stairway leading up to the cabin. They each carried a load of towels and food from the car below. Alice wished she could talk to Emily. She had lots of news to share—about her father, Chance, and writing poetry. But Emily had written only one letter over the course of the summer. It told about hanging out at the mall—and what boys had been there. The letter hadn't even mentioned Alice's poems.

"Hey, what's going on? Where have you guys been?"

Heron. Alice smiled when she recognized the voice. Looking down, she saw Heron's chunky frame charging up the stairs. But Heron looked different this time. Gone was the coal black hair. Heron's hair was bright red! It was brassy and unnatural, and Alice thought it made her look like an old-time movie star.

"We just got back from the beach."

"Cool. Hey, want to go for a hike up Little Creek Road?" Different hair, but same old Heron.

"Mom, can we go for a hike?" Alice called up ahead.

Nora turned. "Aren't you absolutely exhausted after swimming and playing in the waves all day?"

"No, I'm not tired at all. Just a little hungry."

"Okay then. Tell Heron to come inside. We'll cook some hot dogs. Then you two can go for a walk, if you still want to. It'll still be light out for a couple of hours."

Alice got to the top of the hill, set her load down, and pushed the screen door open. "Want to come in and eat?"

"Yeah, I'm starved."

Nora put turkey hot dogs into a saucepan of water and put them on the stove to boil. As Heron entered the small kitchen, Nora noticed her hair. "It looks good," she said. "Different."

"Thanks." Heron fluffed her hair.

"Yeah, looks glamorous," chimed in Alice. Her short brown bob still had sand and salt water in it. She could never get her hair to do anything.

Nora got some hot dog buns and put them on a cookie sheet to warm in the oven. She opened a can of baked beans and made a salad out of fresh lettuce and ripe tomatoes. "Don't you have anyone at home to cook dinner for you, Heron?"

"Not really. My mom works most nights. I usually just snack on whatever stuff we have around. I'm too fat, anyway."

"Oh, baloney," said Nora. "When you're young, like you kids, your bones are growing. You need to eat lots of the right kinds of foods for nourishment. You're not fat. Anyway, you hike all over this place, so you must be in good shape."

Heron grinned. She rolled up the sleeve of her shirt and made a fist. Cocking her elbow, she laughed. "I do have muscles. Nobody better mess with me."

68

"Nobody messes with us girls," chimed in Alice.

Nora laughed, too. "I agree. We women need to stick together."

After they had eaten, Nora shooed them out of the house. "Go for your walk, girls, before it gets dark."

Alice and Heron headed out the back door and started down an old trail that climbed sideways across the mountain. They took a shortcut through the woods, crossing Fox Creek on a fallen log. They scrambled up a steep bank of sword ferns, sprinted across a flat saddle of oak, fir, and madrone, and slid down through a bank of coyote brush onto Little Creek Road.

Alice watched a hawk soar lazily above, riding the evening wind. *He can see everything from way up there,* she thought. *He can see Fox Creek and Little Creek and Baird's Creek and Jacobs Creek, all of them together. He can see the whole picture in his head. See the patterns that they make, running their ragged way down the mountains toward the river and then to the ocean, just like they are supposed to.* She wished that she could see her life like that. She wondered where they would be next year. Would they stay in Fox Creek?

"I guess I really do have a dad," she finally shared with Heron. Kicking rocks out of their path, they walked back lazily on a dirt road that led toward the cabin.

"Of course, you have a dad. Where is he? What did your mom say?"

"Well, that he was tall."

"That's all?"

"Yeah. Well, she said his name is Harold. And that he wasn't very nice to her." Alice was still trying to sort out the things that her mother had told her. "She said that they were in love once, a long time ago."

"Yeah, that's how it always happens. You fall in love, and then presto, there's kids. And then presto, there's no dad, and you gotta work all the time. Or worse, you've got a dad like mine. And then you *wish* there was no dad," said Heron. "I'm never having kids."

"Don't you want to fall in love someday, though?"

"Heck, no. I'm never getting married and never having kids. I'm going to run a karate school. Boom—take that." Heron slashed her foot out sideways, kick-boxing an imaginary opponent. They walked along in silence for a while as evening crept up slowly through the trees.

"So, at least now you know," Heron finally said. "About your dad."

"Yeah." Alice didn't feel that good about knowing. It was still a tender subject. She wanted to talk about something else. "Hey, you know the little dog that's been sleeping under the store?"

"What dog? " asked Heron.

Alice was almost afraid to say. Afraid to jinx it. She hadn't told anyone else about Chance. Well, she had told Ned, but that didn't count. "It's a girl dog. I've been taking her food. Somebody must have dumped her off, 'cause she's real hungry all the time. I think she might be going up to the birthing tree and scratching around in there."

"Are you serious?"

"Well, something's been scratching around in there. I think it might be Chance."

Heron looked puzzled. "Chance?"

"Yeah, that's what I named her. It's like she barely has a chance in life. Well, at least I'm trying to give her a chance."

"Cool," said Heron. "Hey, why don't you leave some food up at the birthing tree. See if she comes up there and gets it."

"That's a great idea," said Alice. "I should have thought of that."

"Maybe we can get one more hot dog apiece from your mom. She'll just think we're really hungry. We'll take the hot dogs outside to eat, but actually we'll save them for your dog. What do you think?"

"My dog?" Alice hadn't allowed herself to think of it that way before. Well, maybe she had thought it, but she hadn't said it out loud. Besides, Alice didn't know if they could afford all this extra food for a dog. Especially one that didn't really belong to her—yet. "I'm not sure if Mom will believe us," she said. "I've already been getting bacon and old bread from my mom. I told her it was to catch crawdads."

"Oh," said Heron. "Well, how about if I just play it up and act super hungry, and she'll feel sorry for me."

"Good plan," said Alice. "Play it up really good, okay? The poor girl who's home alone all the time and whose mother doesn't even feed her."

"Knock it off," said Heron. "Okay, it's true. She doesn't feed us—she's too busy working." But Heron was laughing as she said it. "Come on, race you back."

CHAPTER FOURTEEN

Visiting Heron

*D*ear Emily,

Guess what? We finally went to the beach, and the water was warm. There were big waves and lots of surfers.

Chance lets me pet her a little bit now. She even licked my hand once. Maybe my mom will let me keep her. But right now she is a big secret.

Have you been to any movies this summer? There is no movie theater in this town, but we are going to the drive-in over in Forest Glade on Friday. I have never been to one, have you? Heron and I are going with my mom and Ned (the librarian).

I think my mom likes Ned. That's her big secret, though.

Well, gotta go.

Your friend (still),
Alice

It was deep into summer before Alice saw where Heron lived. Nora had this silly rule about having to meet the parents of Alice's friends before she was allowed to go to their homes. But Heron's mother was never available. She was always working.

On a hot August morning, the timing was right. Nora and Alice drove into town for groceries at Duncan's market and then stopped at the post office before heading home. More than two people in the small place filled it up, so Nora couldn't help it when she literally bumped into a tall, buxom woman with bouffant hair. "Oh, sorry," Nora said as she reached into the box to get their mail.

"Hey, no problem. We're squished like sardines in here." The woman wore tight, stretchy floral pants and a shiny white top, cut low in the front. And right next to her was Heron.

Florence, the postmistress, beamed a broad smile and aimed a finger toward each of them. "Nora," she said, "this is Helen Gunterson. She lives down by the river, raises her brood on a waitress's salary, and is one hardworking gal, let me tell you."

Nora turned towards the woman. "Then you must be Heron's mother," she said. "She's been up at our cabin quite a bit this summer."

Alice grinned at Heron.

"Ohhhh. You're the writer who moved into that cabin up on the hill. The Cooper cabin," said Helen. Her smile was large and genuine. "Good to know you. I tell you, we've been so busy over at the restaurant this summer, I've just been meeting myself coming and going. I'm glad

that you've been watching out for Heron. She never was much one to stay home."

"Well, she's more than welcome anytime," said Nora. "She's been good company for Alice this summer. Is it okay with you if she goes to the movies with us this weekend?"

"Yup. That's just fine. I hear you're going with Ned."

Nora looked perplexed.

"I mean to the movies," Helen continued, winking at Florence, as if they were sharing some private joke. "Although if you ask me, you two are perfect for each other."

Alice watched her mother's face. It was turning three shades of red. She figured it was a good time to change the subject. "Mom, can I go over to Heron's house now that you've met her mom?"

"Well, I don't know.... How will you get home?"

"Walk. Like I always do." *And I can feed Chance on the way back.* She scrunched up her face and pantomimed the word to her: *Pleeaase...*

Heron's mother chimed in. "I'm on my way to work right now, girls, but it's fine with me," she said. "And Heron, you need to clean up your room. Remember?"

Nora glanced around, clearly outnumbered. "Okay," she relented. "But I want you home no later than five, so we can start dinner."

"Boy," said Alice, as she and Heron walked together down the small lane that led toward the river. "You'd think I was a giant, first-class baby, the way she treats me. My mom always has to know exactly where I am ALL the time. Like I'm going to get lost or something."

"Oh well, at least you're coming over," said Heron.

"You can help me bleach my hair. I decided I want to be blonde when we go back to school this year."

"Blonde? What color is your hair really?" asked Alice.

"I don't know. I don't even remember."

"Seriously?"

"Yeah. Well, I think maybe it's dark brown, with a little red in it," said Heron.

"I've just got this plain hair," said Alice. "Plain brown. I'd be totally chicken to try a new color."

The small, modest houses on Heron's lane were built for mill workers, back when the lumber mill was still in operation. Some of them were neat, clean, and tidy, with well-tended gardens and freshly mowed lawns. Others had junky mattresses and garbage piled in their front yards alongside old cars and trucks that didn't run anymore. The houses were laid out on several blocks along a small, flat plain that sat close to the river. Because there were few trees to shade the houses, most of the windows and doors were thrown open wide to capture any slight bit of breeze that might help blow away the suffocating afternoon heat.

Now Alice understood why Heron was such a frequent visitor to their cabin. On Alice's hill, the tall stands of redwood, the spreading oak, and the red-barked madrone seemed cool and inviting compared to these cracker-box houses along the river. She didn't say it, but she liked her cabin a lot better than Heron's.

"Hey, there's my cat," called Heron. "Hey, Stump. Come here, big boy."

Alice's eyes widened. "Wow. That's the *biggest* cat I've ever seen."

CHAPTER FIFTEEN
Hair Scare

Perched on the porch of Heron's plain blue house sat an enormous black and white cat. He was so huge that he almost looked like a statue. He was almost as big as Chance. And where a long, fluffy tail should have been, he had only a rounded stump. "Wow, is that the kitten that you found in the birthing tree?"

"Yup. That's him. I raised him on an eyedropper. And then he started drinking milk. And then, when he started eating real food, he just grew and grew and grew." Heron cuddled the cat next to her, rubbing her face in his soft fur.

Alice reached a hand out to stroke the massive cat. His fur was soft, and his motor was running. You could hear him purring from miles away.

Alice stepped inside the door. The furniture was not very fancy, but everything was arranged in a neat and orderly fashion. Except for Heron's room. The bed was unmade, with piles of clothes dumped on it. Almost every available space on the floor and dresser was littered with soda cans, hair brushes, dishes of food, and cat toys.

78

"Geez. Maybe you'd better clean your room," said Alice.

"Yeah, later." Heron rested on the bed, rubbing Stump on his belly, while he played idly with the strands of her bright red hair.

"So, are you ready?" asked Heron, springing off the bed.

"For what?" Alice followed Heron into her mother's bathroom.

"To help me with my hair," said Heron.

"What do I have to do? I don't know very much about hair."

Heron was digging around in the cabinet under the sink. She pulled out a package and ripped it open. "I'm just gonna mix these two little tubes together, and then I want you to make sure that all of the strands of my hair are covered."

Alice held her nose as Heron prepared the bleach solution. "Yuck," she stated. "Are you sure that stuff is good for your hair?"

"Yeah, I've dyed it before. No problem."

Alice had a bad feeling about all this, but then, Heron was a year older. "So, are you gonna be in seventh grade this year?" Alice asked.

"Nope. I'm gonna be in sixth, just like you. I had to do fifth grade over again, because I skipped so much school. That's when my mom was having all that trouble with my dad coming around drunk and stuff. Things have been better lately, and I went to school a bunch this year. I actually got a B– average," said Heron.

"Where's the school?" asked Alice.

"That building across the river. We're still gonna be in with all the little kids, because it's K to 8. It's not very big—I can practically name every kid in the whole school. The good thing is, in sixth grade they start letting you sign up for classes that you like. You get to take one elective in sixth grade."

"What are you going to take?" asked Alice.

"Karate." Heron spread her feet in a martial arts pose. "Then I can protect myself."

"Cool."

"So, are you and your mom gonna stay in Fox Creek?" asked Heron. She had on rubber gloves and was massaging the smelly solution all over her head. "You've got to register for school soon."

"I don't know yet," said Alice.

"Well, I think you'd better ask your mom," said Heron. "Tell her you want to stay here. Maybe we'll even be in the same class. Hey, how long does the box say to leave this stuff on?"

Alice pinched her fingers against her nose as she dug the box of bleach out of the trash. She read the directions. "It says 10 to 15 minutes, depending upon the desired shade. I'm sort of afraid to bother my mom about school," said Alice. "She's totally involved in finishing her book right now. Plus, we only have the Cooper cabin for the summer. I don't know how much longer we can stay up there." Alice shrugged her shoulders as if in defeat. She couldn't bear the thought of moving again, not even back to Portland.

"Well, I think you should talk to her," said Heron. "I mean, it's your life, too. You asked her about your dad, and you finally found out something, didn't you?"

"Yes," Alice said slowly.

"Well, you'd better say something quick, 'caus
school is going to start in a few more weeks," sai
Heron.

"I'm going to enter the poetry contest at the library,
said Alice. She hadn't really decided until just now
Saying the words out loud seemed to make the decisio
real, irrevocable. "Ned says he thinks I have a chance.'

"Cool. I hope you win something. Then I'll know
famous poet."

"I've got to copy all my poems neatly and turn them
in by the 25th. There's even cash prizes," said Alice.

"So, what are you gonna do with all the money tha
you win?" asked Heron.

"Well, I've been thinking about that," said Alice
"The thing I would buy first is a collar for Chance. Sh
lets me pet her now, and I think she might let me get
collar around her neck. Then I could get her a name tag
so she wouldn't be lost anymore. And I'd buy her som
dog food."

"And then, you'd have a dog, so you'd have to sta
here," said Heron.

"And then we'd have to stay," repeated Alice, as i
saying those words could actually make it happen.

"Hey, this stuff feels really warm," said Heron. "Ho
long has it been on here?"

"I don't know. I didn't look at the time."

"Yeow! It's burning my head," yelped Heron.

CHAPTER SIXTEEN

Making a Decision

*H*eron's hair did not come out blonde. It was a pale, muddy color—like cold oatmeal. It looked awful.

"My mom's gonna kill me," said Heron.

"I hope she's not mad at me, too," said Alice.

"Maybe we didn't leave it on there long enough," Heron said.

"Maybe we left it on too long," said Alice. She was suddenly glad her hair was only plain brown. No hassle.

Heron looked like she was going to cry. "It's gonna look terrible for school," she wailed.

"It looks okay," said Alice, but she didn't look Heron in the eye when she said it. "I'd better go. It'll take a while to walk home." *And I have to check on Chance.* "Besides, you know my mom—Ms. Worrywart."

"Yeah, and I have to clean my room," said Heron. "Come here, Stump." She cradled the big cat against her. "See you."

On her walk home, Alice was struck by how excited and relieved she was to have made up her mind about the poetry contest. Now she would have to decide which poems to choose!

Finally, after several days of thought, Alice picked her five favorite poems and copied them neatly. She tucked them carefully into a large manila envelope, sealed it shut, and kissed it for good luck. Then she walked down Fox Creek Road to the library to turn in her entry, feeling brave and scared at the same time.

She wanted to just lay the envelope down on the counter. She didn't want to talk to anyone. She was afraid it might jinx her chance of winning. But Ned was there, so she handed him the envelope.

"Good for you," he said. "I'm glad you took a chance."

"Thanks," said Alice.

"Hey, I'll pick you and your mom up tonight about 6:30, and then we'll stop and get Heron on the way to the drive-in, okay?"

"Okay, see you tonight." Alice was excited about the movie, but mostly because it would take up time. She had to wait five whole days until they picked the winner of the poetry contest—on August 30. How could she wait five days? After the movie it would only be four days.

Alice headed to the post office to drop off a letter for her mother. She felt like a regular now, because she had been here so much. She noticed that Florence was digging up the pansies and planting chrysanthemums in the old wooden planter outside. "Great flowers," Alice said. "They look good."

"Oh, thank you, dear," said Florence. "My pansies were looking a little ragged here at the end of summer. Chrysanthemums have fall colors—yellow, rust, and

84

gold. They'll look better for autumn, don't you think?"

Autumn! Alice didn't want to think about that. She was still thinking about the next five days of summer. Alice wished summer would last longer. That way, after the poetry contest was over, she would have more time to work with Chance, more time to hike in the forest, more time to walk the creeks, and. . . What if she and her mother left again?

Alice almost didn't hear Florence's next question. "Have you signed up for classes yet?"

"You mean for school?" Alice knew exactly what she meant. She hadn't talked to her mother yet. She hoped that if she didn't say anything at all, maybe things would just go on the way they were. Maybe her mom would just forget all about moving again. Maybe she would fall in love with Ned, and then they might stay in Fox Creek forever. Maybe. . .

"I noticed that sign on the bulletin board." Florence motioned to a large notice on the wall of the post office. "It says that sixth graders need to sign up soon in order to get their choice of electives. Let's see—they're going to offer woodworking, Spanish, karate, and poetry. Are you interested in any of those?"

Alice didn't answer. A lump formed in her throat. Of course, she'd like to take poetry or maybe Spanish. But what was the point? No sense getting excited about things. *We'll probably just move again, right in the middle of it.* All of Alice's feelings—about moving, making friends, and being able to make her own choices in life— just stuck in her craw. "I don't know," she choked, but it came out a mumbled mess. She bounded over all three steps at once and headed toward Duncan's market.

The weather was cooler today. A stiff breeze blew, quite a change from the typical summer heat. Almost as if a storm was coming in. Alice scouted the musty space under the back stairs of the grocery store. "Here, girl. Come on out, little dog," she called.

Where was she? Chance's condition had improved with the daily feedings. The hard edges of her ribs were gone, and her belly was rounding out. But Alice hadn't fed the dog since yesterday, and she must be hungry by now. What would happen to her at the end of the summer? Who would take care of her if Alice and her mom left?

Alice called again. Nothing. The dog wasn't around.

If only there were someone to talk to! Someone who would listen and not ask questions that Alice had no answers for. She had to find Chance.

She longed for the dog's warm nose against her hand. She wanted the dog to sit next to her. She needed to tell Chance something important. She needed to tell her that her mother was almost done with her book about Scotland. That Nora was already talking about the next book and acting restless.

Old Payson came out of the store, clutching a sack of groceries tight against his barrel-like chest.

"Have you seen Chance? The little white dog?" she asked.

"Oh, did you give that mutt a name? Haven't seen the little mongrel—not today, anyway. Mr. Duncan's mighty upset the dog's still hanging out under the store. He says he's going to call the pound pretty soon if someone doesn't claim her."

86

CHAPTER SEVENTEEN

The Drive-In

*H*e can't do that!" cried Alice. Chance was just beginning to trust her. How would the dog feel if someone put a noose around her neck and dragged her to a waiting cage? "I'll go tell him right now. Tell him that. . . "

"Mr. Duncan's not in there today. It's his day off. If that dog's still here tomorrow, though. . . " Payson shuffled toward the post office, clasping his groceries as a brisk wind swirled around him. The clouds appeared darker overhead, and the air smelled heavy.

"I wonder where she could be," said Alice. "It looks like it's going to rain."

"Nah, no need to worry about that. It never rains in California. Not in the summer, anyway."

Alice hung around the store for a while, whistling for the dog. The wind was definitely picking up, sweeping up dust and the stale leaves of summer and blowing them in little whirlwinds throughout the parking lot.

I've got to start for home soon. Ned's coming to pick us up. Alice considered going home the back way to see if Chance had been to the birthing tree, but she had already wasted too much time searching near the market.

Dejected and stung with defeat, Alice shoved half of a sandwich under the edge of the building, hoping Chance would find it later. As she trudged back along Fox Creek Road, the wind pushed her along, blowing hard. It whooshed and whirled, picking up a whole slew of brittle madrone leaves and tossing them in her path. The sky had darkened with the gathering clouds, and the air was heavy.

Alice began to feel uneasy. A hard gust of wind ruffled the sleeves of her shirt and almost lifted her off the road. Relief washed over her when the curving stone stairway came into view. Nora's car was parked down below, and Alice took the broad steps leading up to the cabin two at a time.

"Honey, I'm so glad you're back," said Nora, as she held the door open for Alice. "The way this wind picked up had me worried." With her fingers, she brushed Alice's hair back out of her eyes.

This usually bugged Alice, but right now she didn't care. She was relieved to be safe and home. "Are we still going to the movies?" she asked.

"As far as I know."

"It looks like it's going to rain," said Alice, "but Mr. Payson said it never rains here in the summer."

"Well, he ought to know. He's been here a long time. This is probably a false alarm. It doesn't rain this time of year. That's why everything is so dry and dusty. Don't you remember Oregon?" Nora got a wistful look on her face. "Every so often, we'd get a little rain in the summer. Kept things green and pretty."

"I remember," said Alice. "Are we going back. . . ? "

Alice almost had the question out of her mouth when the phone rang. It was Ned. He would be over to pick them up in about 30 minutes. Alice ate a grilled cheese sandwich in the small kitchen, while Nora got ready.

Nora took a long time in the bathroom, putting on more makeup than usual. She fixed her hair up special with a curling iron, and she kept fussing and fussing with it. *Maybe if I don't say anything about it, she'll just forget all about moving somewhere else.*

Ned came to the door, just like a real gentleman. He held their elbows as they braced themselves against the stiff wind that blew as they descended the rock stairway. The force of the wind made it difficult to open the car door. Alice was used to sitting up front with her mom. But Ned held open the back door for her, and she slipped in behind Nora.

As they drove down Fox Creek Road, Alice couldn't see much out the front window. Just the back of Nora's head. And the back of Ned's. So she occupied herself by gazing into the bushes alongside the road, hoping for a glimpse of Chance. Alice felt guilty leaving her out in the storm. But it wasn't really going to rain, was it?

As they drove through the rows of plain clapboard houses along the river, Alice saw Heron waiting outside on her front porch. Stump was sprawled across her shoulders like a fur collar. Alice hadn't seen her for a few days—not since the disaster with the bleach mix.

Heron shook the cat loose and, kissing him, gently set him on the porch rocker. Something was different about her. Ned helped her with the door, and as she clambered into the backseat, Alice saw what it was.

90

"How did you do that?" said Alice. "Your hair looks the way it used to."

"My mom helped me," said Heron. "She wasn't mad at all. In fact, I think she felt sorry for me. She had a friend of hers do a weave on it. They mixed brown and a little red together." She combed through her hair with her fingers. "Do you think it looks okay?"

"Yeah, it looks great," said Alice.

"Looks fine to me," said Ned.

"I like this color better than anything else I've seen on you," said Nora, turning around with a smile.

It was about 12 miles to the drive-in movie at Forest Glade. Ned drove cautiously, with both hands gripping the steering wheel. The wind blew so hard that trees on the side of the road seemed to tilt horizontally. Heron found this hysterical. "Watch out. It's a hurricane," she laughed as she tilted against Alice in the backseat.

Alice couldn't help but giggle. Soon they were both careening sideways in the backseat, mimicking the movement of the trees outside their windows.

Nora turned to Ned. "Do you think they will even show the movie if it starts raining?"

"I don't think it's actually going to rain," said Ned. "I've never seen it rain here in the summer, and I've lived here my whole life. This is quite a wind storm we're having, though."

Where would a dog find shelter in a wind storm? Even with the laughter and excitement of the evening, something inside of Alice couldn't let go of her concern about Chance. The dog had become a part of her now.

CHAPTER EIGHTEEN

Raining Cats and Dogs

Watching the movie at the old drive-in was not what Alice had expected at all. They drove the car up close to a metal post, where they found a speaker that was attached by a wire. They pulled the speaker into the car and propped it against the rolled-up window, but it sounded scratchy and made everyone laugh. They could still hear the wind whistling through the partly open window.

"There's not very many people here," said Nora.

"Yeah, it's kinda spooky," said Heron.

"*WuuuHuuu, WuuuHuuu,*" said Ned, in a scary voice.

Alice and Heron burst into a fit of laughter in the backseat. Soon the show began and all four of them quieted down and became absorbed in the action. Alice noticed that Ned let his arm rest on the seat behind her mom's head. Nora didn't seem to mind. In fact, she laid her head back against his arm for a while.

Even by the end of the movie, the wind had not relented. On the curving road back to Fox Creek, it felt as if a monsoon was arriving. "This is crazy weather," said Ned. "It even smells like rain."

Alice peered out the car window. In the darkness she could see nothing except the ghostly silhouettes of trees swaying back and forth on the side of the road. When a few small raindrops hit the windshield, she sang out with surprise, "Look, it's raining. In the summer."

As they came around the last bend before town, Ned slowed the car. "Do you need anything at the store?"

Alice's heart skipped a beat. She could check on Chance!

"No, I think we're fine on groceries," said Nora.

Alice cut in, thinking fast. "No, we need milk, Mom. I drank up almost all of it with dinner."

"Are you sure? Okay, we may as well stop, so we'll have some for morning."

With the force of the wind, it took both hands for Ned to open the car door for Nora. He escorted her into the market and held open the heavy glass entry door.

Alice and Heron scampered out of the car. The parking lot was still dusty. It had been a long time since it had rained. Heron tipped her head backwards, facing the sky and tasting the rain on her tongue. "Delicious," she said. She held her hands out and appeared to be doing a rain dance.

Alice was amused at her friend's antics, but she snuck quickly around the corner to the side of the small market. "Chance," she called out. "Where are you, girl?"

"What are you doing?" Heron appeared from behind her, wiping the raindrops off her face.

"Looking for Chance. She's not here."

"She's probably all curled up somewhere else, warm and cozy," said Heron. "She'll be okay."

"But I left half of my roast beef sandwich for her this afternoon." Alice pointed towards the uneaten food. "See? It's still there. It hasn't even been touched. What if something's happened to her?"

Alice heard her mother's voice. "Come on, girls. Get back in the car. Hurry."

The wind blew the raindrops sideways in heavy gusts. Alice and Heron scrambled into the backseat.

Ned drove Heron home and waited to make sure that she was safely in the door. Then they drove to Alice and Nora's small cabin on the hill.

"I'd better walk you up," said Ned.

The raindrops had now become larger, as if the sky was really going to open up and pour. Alice ducked inside the house, and Ned and Nora stood in the doorway for a long time, talking. Alice wondered what they were saying to each other, but she didn't want to spy on them. Instead she was thinking about Chance. *Where could she have gone in this storm?*

"You'd better get home, Ned," she heard her mom say, "before you can't even see the road."

"Yeah, I guess you're right," laughed Ned. "This feels like a bad storm. Doesn't seem like August at all. It's really getting nasty out there."

Alice peeked out the window as she got ready for bed. She watched Ned make his way carefully down the stone staircase, slippery now with the steadily increasing rain. Mother Nature must be laughing at all those people who think they can predict the weather—the ones who say it never rains in California in the summertime. *Well, it's pouring out there now.*

Nora came in to Alice's small bedroom to say good night. It reminded Alice of when she was a little girl, still getting tucked into bed. "Be glad that you have a nice warm place to sleep tonight," said Nora. "It's raining cats and dogs out there."

Why did she have to say that? Alice pulled the quilt up over her head, nestling into the warmth. It was cozy in her bed, but Alice couldn't get comfortable. A loud clap of thunder brought her instantly to her senses. Peeking out from under the covers, she saw a flash of lightning out her window. Alice sat straight up, wide awake now.

Where was Chance? She didn't have a nice warm place to sleep. She was out in the storm somewhere. Probably scared out her wits, shivering and cold.

She sat on the edge of her bed, trying to arrive at a decision. It was stormy outside, but Alice had been in lots of rainstorms when they lived in Oregon. The fierce wind howled outside her window, but there was no point in going back to bed. She knew that she wasn't going to sleep as long as she was worried about Chance.

Alice heard the thunder again. It was louder this time, ricocheting off the mountain behind the cabin. Her mind became focused, and she knew what she had to do. Without turning on the light, Alice rummaged in her closet until she found the warm, hooded jacket that she had brought with her from Oregon. She pulled on heavy socks and laced her sneakers on. Moving in slow motion, she edged her bedroom door open so that she wouldn't disturb her mother.

Creeping into the darkened back room, Alice didn't turn on the light. She heard a scraping sound against the window, and she stopped dead in her tracks. With her heart pounding against her chest, she tried to reassure herself that it was just the wind. Alice almost lost her nerve, but she had to find Chance. The little dog needed her. She knew it. She could feel it.

Alice used her fingertips to search along the ledge by the back door. The flashlight! She had hoped it would be there. Alice grasped it tightly in her fist as she pushed the screen door open. Bracing herself against the howling wind, she stepped out of the warmth of the cabin and into the relentless rain.

Finding Puppie.

*T*he rain began to beat against Alice's body as sh
moved toward the stone stairway. The steps were slicl
the wind intense. Alice cast the flashlight from side to sid
in front of her. Planting one foot down and then regainir
her balance before she proceeded with the next foot mad
the going slow. Finally, she reached the clearing at th
bottom and made her way toward Fox Creek Road.

Alice knew about rain—she had lived in Oregon. Th
weather there changed frequently, and it was ofte
unpredictable. So it wasn't the actual rain in Alice's fac
that troubled her. It was the shape of the trees lurkin
along the side of the road. And it was the dank, ra
smell of the parched forest as it sucked in the welcomin
rain like a person dying of thirst. Alice thought abou
crawling back into her warm bed, but she was alread
cold and wet. The idea that Chance might be all alone an
lost in this storm gave her courage. She had to keep goin

Alice usually had no trouble finding the secret tra
that led down past the birthing tree. But the rain, whic
at first had simply washed the dust from the leaves an
brightened the narrow path, was now beating dow

98

the tree limbs on either side. It lay a heavy hand on the overhanging oak and madrone, and it slashed at the underbrush on each side of the narrow opening. Even the stately redwoods seemed dark and forboding, and what was once familiar to her now looked strange and menacing. But Alice gathered the hood of her jacket together at her throat and pressed on.

She remembered how excited she had been when Heron first showed her this trail through the woods. How captivated she had been by its beauty. How she had sat and written poems about the forest from the sides of this very trail. Now she stumbled along in the darkness, guided only by the thin beam from her flashlight, with a vague sense of where she was going. "Chance?" she called out, but her voice seemed to disappear into the night.

Alice couldn't imagine writing poems about this situation. Unless it was gothic horror poetry. Now she wished that she had never entered the poetry contest. There was no way she would win. They would probably move away soon, anyway.

Unless—Nora fell in love and got married to Ned. *In your dreams. Do you think you're living in a fairy tale?* Alice kept walking, pushing into the wind.

As the rain poured down, the path in front of her became slippery. The dry dust of summer was quickly changing to heavy muck that sucked at the soles of her shoes and made the going difficult. She stumbled along, shining the beam of the flashlight into the undergrowth, trying to keep her sense of direction.

Alice knew she must be getting close, because the trail bent to the left here. The birthing tree was not too far from this spot in the path. It was the only place she could imagine that Chance might be, but it was just a hunch—based on a memory of a white object fleeing from this spot earlier in the summer. Now as she neared the tree, she almost lost her nerve. Everything seemed confused and different in the dark. "Chance, are you here, girl?" she called.

Alice heard a soft whimper. She edged closer. The trees around her shuddered with the force of the wind, and then abruptly the whole sky lit up—bright as daylight. Alice instinctively ducked, as jagged lightning raced across the sky. She stole a glimpse forward. The birthing tree was just ahead. In the blinding glare, she saw a white animal in the hollow of the tree. Was it Chance?

Just as Alice started to call her, a heavy clap of thunder sounded right over her head—so loud that she dropped to the ground in fright. From the corner of her eye, she saw the animal jump out of the birthing tree and run toward the underbrush to hide.

Now Alice was frightened. She had told no one where she was going. *Mom won't even know where to look for me. And lightning strikes high things, like trees.* She had never imagined that this California summer storm could become so dangerous. She had been foolish to come out in a lightning storm.

She had to get out of the forest and away from the tall trees. She stumbled forward, calling for Chance, but she tripped on one of the twisted roots of the old birthing tree. Falling to her knees, she grasped the ancient redwood for balance, barely keeping her grip on the slippery flashlight. Shining it down into the hollow of the tree, she saw something squirming there on the ground. It looked like rats. Alice's heart raced in her chest.

She tried to regain her balance on the uneven ground and felt the warm breath of an animal against her knee. *Chance!* The small wet dog slithered past her and entered the hollowed-out place in the center of the birthing tree. "Chance," she said. "Come here, girl. Please don't go in there with those things."

Alice was trying to stand up, trying to decide what to do, when another jagged bolt of lightning lit the sky. Alice could suddenly see clearly what lay before her in the burned-out old tree, almost as if a street light had been turned on. Chance was licking the squirming creatures, one by one, as if they were the most important things in the world. She was not licking rats, but puppies! Four of them, and they looked as if they had just been born. The tiny things had their eyes tightly closed and hair was matted down against their fragile bodies. Encouraged by the attention of their mother, they wiggled madly against her rough tongue.

The thunder rumbled in the distance. Shining the flashlight back toward the puppies, Alice saw that rain had started to pool in the back of the old, hollow tree. What had been a snug and secure nest for the pups would soon become a flooded quagmire.

Alice took off her heavy jacket. She knotted the arms together and made a soft sling. The rain stung the exposed back of her neck, but she ignored it. Holding the flashlight in the crook of her arm, she carefully picked up each small pup, and she settled them one by one into the warmth of her jacket. Chance became increasingly nervous as her pups disappeared from view. Alice opened the jacket a little, showing Chance the pups, and the white dog nuzzled them with her nose.

Alice felt the chill of the rain settle in against her skin. She rose slowly. Cradling the puppies gently against her body and shining the flashlight onto the muddy trail in front of her, she started toward home. The trail looked different going in this direction, murky and dark. She called for the white dog.

Chance had never followed her before. She had always run away. "Come here, girl. Let's go get your puppies dry." The small dog seemed unsure, looking back toward the birthing tree and into the bushes, as if searching for a place to hide. "Come on, girl. I would never hurt you. Or your puppies. Come on, Chance," Alice called anxiously.

Alice started walking. It was hard for her to hold the flashlight and keep the puppies snug against her at the same time without squishing them. She was cold, and the rain was still beating down. She looked back into the dark night, trying to see if Chance was following. The white dog had to come. She had to learn to trust someone, and she needed to take care of her babies.

Alice didn't see the branch blown down in front of her, and she stumbled. Using both hands to keep the puppies from falling, she felt the flashlight drop out of her hand and bounce away down a steep slope. Alice heard it crashing through the underbrush. She looked behind for Chance. She looked up ahead for the trail. All she could see was darkness.

Finding Chanc

*A*lice squinted through the bushes, trying to mak out an opening that might be the trail. There was onl the barest outline of spooky trees and sodden branche heavy with rain. Her elbow hurt, and she felt mu oozing against her bare skin through the ripped knee c her pants.

Already drenched from the brutal wind and rair Alice could hardly bear the loss of her flashlight. Th puppies whimpered against her chest. Alice wanted t sit down on the trail and cry. She wanted to be rescued She wanted her mother to come.

But Alice knew that wasn't going to happen. Even i her mother awoke and found her gone, how would sh know where to look? Alice sat, alone and wet, on a pitcl black trail with four newborn puppies squirming agains her. She wasn't going to cry. She wasn't. When she fel salty drops of moisture begin edging slowly down he cheek, she told herself it was just the rain.

Alice clung to the puppies. She rocked back an forth, soothing them. They whimpered and wiggled crying for their mother. She wondered how long it woul be before they needed milk. What would she do if Chance ran off, like the wild mother cat had done so long ago? Alice didn't think she could raise four puppies on an eyedropper. They might not make it.

Something cold and clammy pushed against Alice's arm. "Chance," she cried, "you just about scared me to death." Alice cracked her jacket open and Chance stuck her nose inside. The white dog snuffled all four puppies in turn, satisfying herself that each one was all right. Then she pushed her wet body in close to Alice. Alice reached over and held Chance against her.

She stroked the dog's ears and scratched under her chin. Chance responded as if she were remembering some kindness from long ago. A murmuring noise came from deep in her throat, and Chance edged her body closer.

The thunder seemed to be moving off into the distance, on the far side of the crest of mountains. Alice heard it faintly as she felt her exhaustion. The four puppies were quiet and sleeping now. Alice cradled them gently against her as she huddled on the cold forest floor, clinging to a wet and scraggly little dog.

*   *   *   *   *

"Alice, ALICE. Where are you?"

She awoke with a start. Momentarily forgetting where she was, Alice almost dropped the puppies from her jacket. It was totally dark, and Alice could see nothing. Drenched and clammy, she shivered in the cold. Was that a voice?

Chance licked her face and nosed around inside the jacket for the puppies. Alice remembered the storm. She was not sure how long she had been sitting on the trail.

"ALICE, can you hear me?" a man's voice shouted.

Alice felt Chance bristle at the sound of a strange voice. She reached down to soothe the nervous dog. "It's all right, girl," she said. Alice lay her jacket down on the ground and opened it so that Chance could inspect the puppies.

Her joints felt stiff and achy, and her knee throbbed, but Alice stood up. The rain had stopped, but she could see nothing in the dark. "Over here," she yelled into the night. Her voice was shaky. "I'm over here."

She saw a dim light coming through the bushes up ahead. It moved from side to side, searching for her. She called out again, louder this time. "I'm h-e-r-e!"

The light became brighter, and she could make out shapes. "Alice, are you okay?" It was Ned!

Alice leaned over, carefully scooping up the jacket containing the four puppies. Gingerly, she made her way toward the light.

"Alice, are you there?" her mother's voice pleaded. Alice recognized her, coming quickly down the soggy trail. Nora darted in front of Ned and ran toward her daughter, hugging her fiercely.

Alice squirmed sideways out of her grasp. "Be careful, Mom. You'll squish them."

"Squish what? How did you get out here? Have you been here all night? I've been worried half to death."

"I had to come, Mom," said Alice. "I know I'm all wet. But I was looking for. . . "

Her mother wasn't paying attention. "With all that lightning and thunder, I went to look in on you. When you weren't in your bed, I was going to call the police, but then I called Ned. And I called Heron to see if she knew where you could possibly be. She said you were worried about some dog. . . "

"I was finding Chance," said Alice. The small dog paced back and forth anxiously, unsure of what all the commotion meant.

"I didn't know where you were, honey. I was frantic."

"I'm glad you found me, Mom," said Alice. "Chance had puppies in the birthing tree, and then I thought lightning was going to hit it, and we started back towards home, and then I dropped the flashlight, and then. . . "

"And I showed them where the trail was. . . . " Heron popped out of the bushes, just behind Ned.

"Alice, you're lucky we were able to find you at all," said Ned. "You might have been out here all night. I knew you'd been feeding a dog, but Heron put the pieces together for us. She was the one who figured out you might have gone up to the birthing tree, even in this storm."

Alice tried to digest all of this. She was wrung out from all the excitement and from the cold and the rain. The pups squirmed against her, crying. Hearing them whimper, Chance came to her side. "Mom, I'm glad you found me. But we have to get these puppies home so that Chance can nurse them."

"Puppies?"

"Mom, you haven't been listening! Chance had puppies—see?" Alice opened her jacket in the dim light, gauging her mother's reaction to the tiny creatures.

"I guess I didn't realize what you had in there. . . . That's why that stray dog is acting so worried. Now let's get you home, honey. You're sopping wet."

"She's not a stray dog," said Alice. "Her name is Chance." She backed away from her mother, holding the puppies against her defiantly.

"Alice. Come ON! You're cold and almost delirious. You're going to get sick if we don't go back to the cabin and—"

"No, Mom. I don't want to go anywhere." The words seemed to come from some deep place inside of her, welling up and spilling out of their own volition. "I want to stay here—right here in Fox Creek. I don't want to move again."

"Honey, I never said we were moving."

"I know, Mom. You never tell me anything," said Alice. "I'm sick of moving around so much. All my life, we move and move and move again. Always moving. Well, I'm sick of it." Her voice was breaking, and she tried not to cry. Wet and exhausted, she blurted out what she had been wanting to say all summer. "I like it here, because we already have some friends. I want to go to school in Fox Creek. I already know Heron, and I want to meet some other kids here. I want to belong somewhere, Mom. And I want to keep Chance. She's my dog now." Chance was at Alice's side, as if she knew something important was happening.

"Alice, this is no place to make a decision like that. It's dark, and it's cold. We need to get you home. We'll talk about it later."

"Not later," said Alice. "You always say that. Now!

We need to talk about it now!" Alice stood her ground, the dog pressed tightly against her body.

Nora sucked in a breath. Her shoulders moved up and then down again, as she seemed to struggle with her words. "Okay, Alice," she said finally. "Maybe you're right. I honestly didn't know it meant so much to you. Maybe we should stay. We have met some nice people." She glanced up at Ned momentarily. "And it does feel like we almost belong here already. Now please, honey, it's the middle of the night." Nora took a tentative step towards her daughter, her arms open. "Let's get your dog home and find a bed for these little pups. And we need to get you out of your wet clothes before you freeze to death."

Heron led the way down the path, shining the flashlight behind her to light the way for the others. Ned and Nora came next, moving slowly on the uneven terrain and glancing backwards to make sure that Alice was coming.

Alice brought up the rear, moving slowly so as not to disturb her delicate bundle of tiny, wiggly pups. And right by her side was a small white dog, keeping pace with her and glancing up at her from time to time.

CHAPTER TWENTY-ONE

Home at Last

*D*ear Emily,

I've almost been too busy to write. A lot of stuff has happened. I won second place in the poetry contest. My prize was $25.00. Pretty good, huh? The person that beat me is a boy. Can you believe that? His name is Jeremy Suter, and we are both taking poetry this year as an elective.

With my $25.00, I bought Chance a collar, a name tag, and some dog food. Oh yeah, she had four puppies in a big storm. I got lost in the storm, but then everybody found me. Don't let anyone tell you that it never rains in California in the summertime, because believe me, sometimes it does!

Anyway, my mom let me keep Chance, who is getting really tame now. My best friend Heron took one of the pups. She named it Tree, because it was born in the birthing tree like her cat, Stump. I guess that she likes weird names, too.

Mr. Payson took one of the puppies to keep him

111

company. Florence, down at the post office, took one, too. To guard the place, she said.

I have one puppy left. He is black and white and really cute. You should see him play. He growls and barks and chews on things. I'm going to call him Storm. Maybe we will keep him. Then we will have two dogs!

Gotta go now. I've got to drop some books off at the library and then go home, do homework, and play with my dogs. Have a good year at school.

Oh yeah. My mother finished her book. We get to stay in the Cooper cabin for at least a year, until we can find something more permanent. (Maybe my mom and Ned will even get married.) Hope you can visit someday.

Your friend,

Alice
P.S. Here's a poem for you:

With redwoods and creeks that run to the sea
And beaches and waves that crash wild and free,
Who'd ever guess that out of the blue
I'd find a chance to become someone new.
A new state, a cool state
it's taken my heart.
California is my home.